OKLAHOMA

"JOGRAPHY"

A Fun Run Through Our State!

by
Carole Marsh

This activity book has material which correlates with Oklahoma's Priority Academic Student Skills. At every opportunity, we have tried to relate information to the History and Social Science, English, Science, Math, Civics, Economics, and Computer Technology Oklahoma PASS directives. For additional information, go to our websites: **www.oklahomaexperience.com** or **www.gallopade.com**.

Correlates with Oklahoma's PASS Priority Academic Student Skills™

GALLOPADE INTERNATIONAL

Reading · Research · Reinforcement · Reference

Gallopade is proud to be a member of these educational organizations and associations:

SHOPA MEMBER™ School, Home, & Office Products Association

NSSEA

ASCD

The Oklahoma Experience Series

The Oklahoma Experience! Paperback Book

My First Pocket Guide to Oklahoma!

The Big Oklahoma Reproducible Activity Book

The Oklahoma Coloring Book!

My First Book About Oklahoma!

Oklahoma Jeopardy: Answers and Questions About Our State

Oklahoma "Jography!": A Fun Run Through Our State

The Oklahoma Experience! Sticker Pack

The Oklahoma Experience! Poster/Map

Discover Oklahoma CD-ROM

Oklahoma "GEO" Bingo Game

Oklahoma "HISTO" Bingo Game

Table of Contents

What is "Jography"?

Dear Parent, Teacher, Librarian, and other readers,

Haven't you ever heard a kid pronounce geography joooography—as in, "I have lots of 'jography' homework but I left my jooography book at school and we have a jooography test tomorrow!"

From the reports that we read, that kid may very well flunk that "jography" test. What a shame that such a vital, interesting, essential subject has been so short-changed. Why is this? Perhaps we thought geography was boring when we were in school. Maybe it seems to change too much. Just when we figure out where a country is, it changes its name, capital, and government! Or are we not willing or able to visualize the world as what it is—just a big neighborhood?

Whatever the reason, I hope my series of "Jography" books helps make geography more exciting and interesting. Never before has geography been a more important study for students. Through political and environmental concerns, we have found just how important it is for us to know where our neighbors are and what they are up to. And the world is growing economically smaller. A child's future career may take them further than around the block! They are almost bound to be involved with other countries and their language, cultures, and money.

But the best place to start is out our own back door! Perhaps geography does seem boring or useless until someone gives us season passes to our favorite team's games. Then all we have to do is figure out how to get there. Now that's motivation!

So, the approach this book takes is to consider geography from the kid's point of view—what they may be interested in, plus to communicate that geography is history, economics, politics, art, science, communication, etc.

Thank you for helping kids get hooked on "jography"!

Carole Marsh

Some Down-To-Earth Reasons to Know Your "Jography"

Recent studies show most people know very little about the places in the world in which they live.

Sometimes it's as important to know where somewhere isn't, as much as where it is (unless you like catching the right plane to the wrong destination or vice versa!).

If you don't want to learn too much about a place, at least hit the high spots so you won't sound dumb or insult someone. But even more importantly, go ahead and learn a lot about a place you're interested in. After all, in today's truly global economy, there's just no telling where in the world you'll find yourself calling on the phone, putting money in the bank, or traveling to by plane, boat, or rickshaw!

What's "Jography"? It's a way to explore a place that's just a little more realistic and a little more fun. Most people don't even know much about the geography of their state until someone gives them free tickets to the big game—now all they have to do is figure out how to get there! And I'll bet if they announced there was money growing on trees in Kalamazoo, you'd have no trouble finding out exactly where it is!

So, put on your jogging shoes, lace 'em up tight and let's go on an armchair journey. Like any true traveler and serious geographer—of course you can use a map! Look in an encyclopedia, atlas, or ask your parent or teacher until you find a map that you like and that makes sense to you. Then see if you find the answers to some of the following questions. I'll bet you discover them and a whole lot more!

Happy "Jographing"! And for fun—keep score!

Oklahoma

"Jography" Word Search

Before you get started, jog your memory! You've heard of most of the geography-related words below. Find them in this word search. Hint: You'll only find them by latitude and longitude! Score one point for each word discovered.

```
C H A R T X L I D E G R E E O C E A N
O P O L E Z R H E Q U A T O R X B M N
N D G L A C I E R X U I S L A N D N B
T E M O U N T A I N R U Y L A K E M O
I S A R C T I C P L C I V O L M R J A
N E R I V E R X J O V W I N D U R P C
E R T D E L T A Z N E G L O B E M R S
N T I Z O N E L M G R V O L C A N O X
T R O P I C S X C I B E A R T H M A P
G L V J S B V M K T I D E W A T E R L
V V A P S L P P L U C L W Q P M F C A
D U B L A T I T U D E P I E D M O N T
P T N A L L X I N E W Z M R P O I U E
O G R I D E V K J H R E G I O N S P A
X P E N I N S U L A M N B C X H G E U
```

Word Bank

CHART DEGREE OCEAN POLE LATITUDE EQUATOR GLACIER ISLAND
MOUNTAIN LAKE ARCTIC WIND DELTA GLOBE ZONE VOLCANO
TROPICS EARTH CONTINENT DESERT RIVER LONGITUDE TIDEWATER
PIEDMONT PLAIN PENINSULA GRID PLATEAU REGIONS MAP

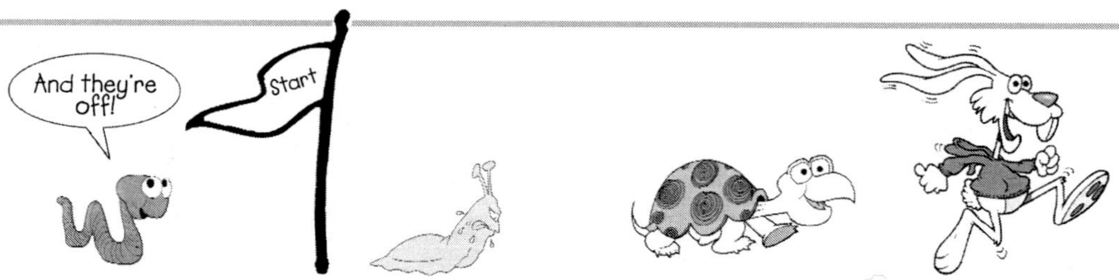

MY SCORE ______

Oklahoma "Jography" Comes in All Flavors!

Match the type of geography with the area of study it would cover. Score one point for each correct answer. Be sure to cover the bottom of the sheet until you have your answers!

Branch		Study	
1.	Geography	A.	Land forms
2.	Physiography	B.	Weather forecasting
3.	Mathematical geography	C.	The physical Earth
4.	Biogeography	D.	People and geography
5.	Oceanography	E.	Plants, animals
6.	Meteorology	F.	Parallels, meridians
7.	Economic geography	G.	Waves, tides, currents
8.	Anthropography	H.	Industry location
9.	Climatology	I.	Government boundaries
10.	Political geography	J.	Weather

MY SCORE ______

ANSWERS: 1-C; 2-A; 3-F; 4-E; 5-G; 6-B ; 7-H; 8-D; 9-J; 10-I

Oklahoma

Our State from A-To-Z!

This should give you a good overview of your state. Take your map and see if you can find a mountain, river, or place for each letter of the alphabet listed here. Score one point for each. (Score two points if you find a Q, U, X, Y, Z!)

A______________________________
B______________________________
C______________________________
D______________________________
E______________________________
F______________________________
G______________________________
H______________________________
I______________________________
J______________________________
K______________________________
L______________________________
M______________________________
N______________________________
O______________________________
P______________________________
QUICK, YOU'RE DOING GREAT!__________
R______________________________
S______________________________
T______________________________
U CAN DO IT!____________________
V______________________________
W______________________________
X______________________________
Y______________________________
Z______________________________

MY SCORE ______

Oklahoma

A-Maze-ing Capital!

__ __ __ __ __ __ __ __   __ __ __ __ is the capital city of Oklahoma. Can you find your way through the maze to the capitol building? Score 10 points when you arrive!

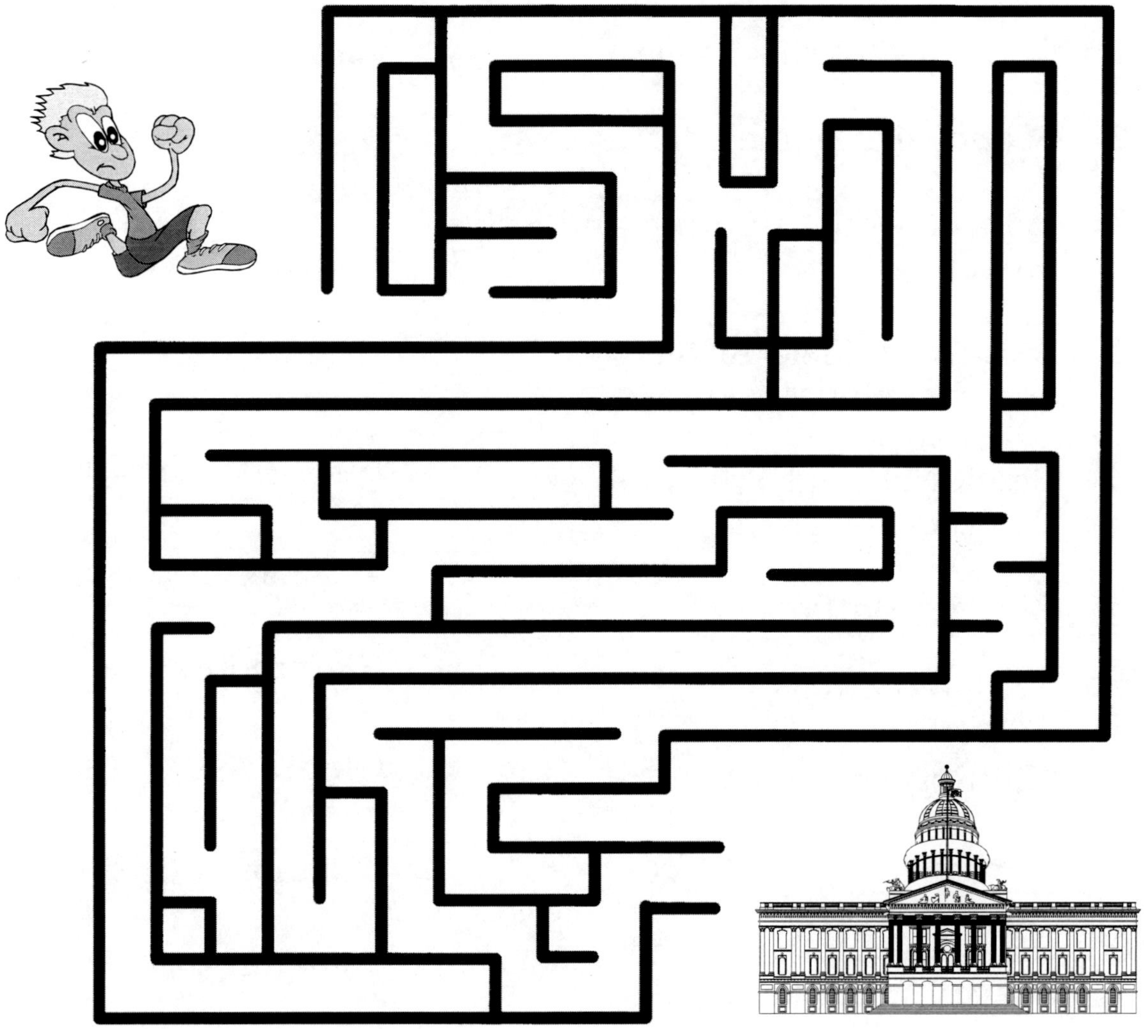

ANSWER: Oklahoma City

MY SCORE ______

Oklahoma

The Great Escape!

Hop on your bike and take a tour of these Oklahoma landmarks and attractions. Score a point for each place you can match correctly.

Yikes! Bike Tour

1. Cathedral of the Osage
2. Sequoyah's home
3. Pioneer Woman Statue and Museum
4. U.S. Army Field Artillery and Fort Sill Museum
5. Creek National Tribal Complex
6. Washita Battlefield
7. Woolaroc Museum
8. Will Rogers Memorial
9. Cherokee Heritage Center
10. Oklahoma Aviation and Space Hall of Fame

A. Sallisaw

B. Lawton

C. Ponca City

D. Bartlesville

E. Northwest of Cheyenne

F. Tahlequah

G. Claremore

H. Okmulgee

I. Oklahoma City

J. Pawhuska

ANSWERS: 1-J; 2-A; 3-C; 4-B; 5-H; 6-E; 7-D; 8-G; 9-F; 10-I

MY SCORE ______

Oklahoma

Over the River and Through the Woods!

See if you can figure out which Oklahoma river, lake, mountains, or forest we're looking for—and score one point for each one you match!

Keep an Eye to the Sky!

1. Arkansas River
2. Red River
3. Wichita Mountains
4. Black Kettle National Grasslands
5. Ouachita National Forest
6. Keystone Reservoir
7. Ozark Mountains
8. Tallgrass Prairie Preserve
9. Arbuckle Mountains
10. Eufaula Lake

A. Mountain range in the southwest

B. Forest in southeastern Oklahoma

C. Man-made lake near Tulsa

D. Mountains in southern Oklahoma

E. Forms the southernmost border with Texas

F. Flows south through eastern Oklahoma

G. Preserved prairie landscape, near Pawhuska

H. Mountain range in northeastern Oklahoma

I. Largest lake in Oklahoma

J. Grasslands in western Oklahoma

MY SCORE ______

ANSWERS: 1-F; 2-E; 3-A; 4-J; 5-B; 6-C; 7-H; 8-G; 9-D; 10-I

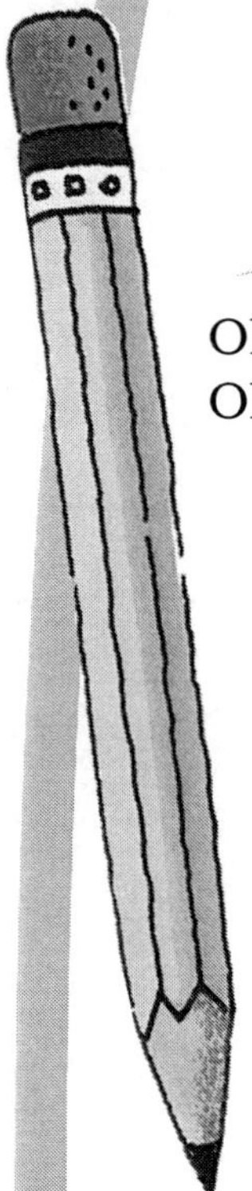

Oklahoma

State Borders

Oklahoma is surrounded by other states and a body of water. Can you name Oklahoma's borders? Score one point for each item you match.

North to South and East to West!

1. Colorado	A. The Land of Enchantment to the west
2. Kansas	B. Neighbor to the north, home of Topeka
3. Texas	C. Lone Star State to the south
4. New Mexico	D. Land of Opportunity to the east
5. Arkansas	E. The number of bordering states around Oklahoma
6. Missouri	F. Neighbor to the northwest, home to Denver
7. Red River	G. Flows between Oklahoma and part of Texas
8. Six	H. Northeastern neighbor, home to St. Louis

MY SCORE ______

ANSWERS: 1-F; 2-B; 3-C; 4-A; 5-D; 6-H; 7-G; 8-E

Oklahoma

A Few of My Favorite Things and Places

I'll bet they are yours too! But where in the world are they?!
Score one point for each riddle you solve.

Fun! Fun! Fun! Fun!

1. I am where Indian City U.S.A. recreates Plains living.
   I am about 35 miles (56 kilometers) north of Fort Sill.
   Where am I? ______________________

2. I sprang up overnight in 1901 as a result of the last land run.
   I am the third largest city in Oklahoma.
   Where am I? ______________________

3. The Santa Fe Railroad helped me grow and develop.
   I am home to the Oklahoma Sooners.
   Where am I? ______________________

4. My name means "bubbling water" in the Creek language.
   I am where the Black Invitational Rodeo is held.
   Where am I? ______________________

5. The Arkansas, Verdigris, and Grand rivers meet near me.
   I was founded in 1872 on the Old Texas Road.
   Where am I? ______________________

ANSWERS: 1-Anadarko; 2-Lawton; 3-Norman; 4-Okmulgee; 5-Muskogee

MY SCORE ______

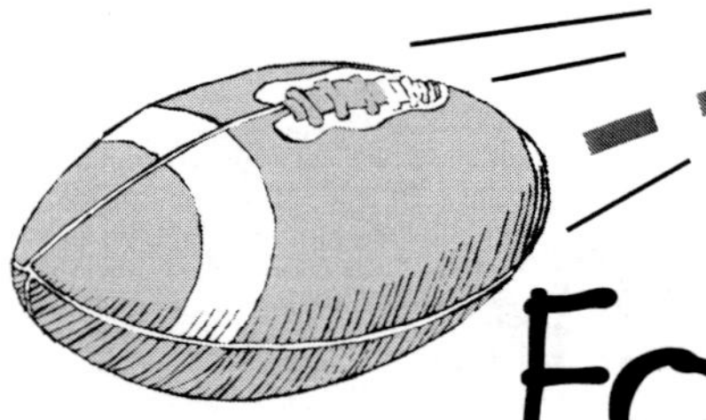

Oklahoma Football Fever!

If someone gave you season tickets to a game or activity of the schools below—would you know where to find them? Score a point for each school and town you match.

Rah! Rah!! Rah!!!

1. University of Oklahoma
2. Oklahoma State University
3. University of Central Oklahoma
4. Southwestern Oklahoma State University
5. Phillips University
6. Oral Roberts University
7. Oklahoma Baptist University
8. Oklahoma Panhandle State University
9. University of Science and Arts of Oklahoma
10. Oklahoma City University

A. Stillwater
B. Weatherford
C. Tulsa
D. Chickasha
E. Norman
F. Shawnee
G. Edmond
H. Goodwell
I. Oklahoma City
J. Enid

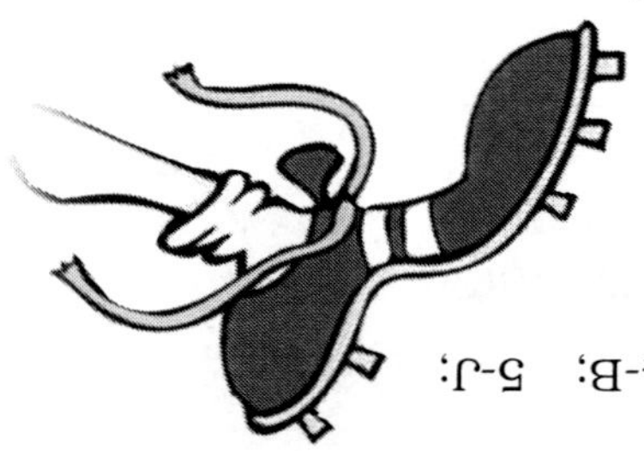

ANSWERS: 1-E; 2-A; 3-G; 4-B; 5-J; 6-C; 7-F; 8-H; 9-D; 10-I

MY SCORE ______

Oklahoma Road Rally!

This is like a scavenger hunt by car! Here are the places on your list. Score one point for each name you complete.

RRRROAD RRRRALLY!

1. A furry animal that builds dams: _ _ _ _ _ _
2. He is married to the queen: _ _ _ _ ston
3. A large woolly plains animal: _ _ _ _ _ _ _
4. Tie a lot of this to your kite: _ _ _ _ _ _ town
5. Yellow kernels on a cob: _ _ _ _
6. Moisture on the grass in the morning: _ _ _ ey
7. An instrument played by beating with a stick: _ _ _ _ right
8. A small wild horse of the southwestern plains: _ _ _ _ _ _ _
9. It's the opposite of bad: _ _ _ _ well
10. "Moo" says this milk producer: _ _ _ lington

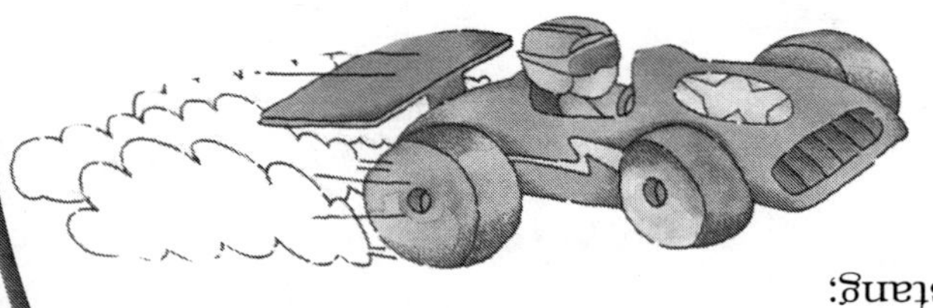

ANSWERS: 1-Beaver; 2-Kingston; 3-Buffalo; 4-Stringtown; 5-Corn; 6-Dewey; 7-Drumright; 8-Mustang; 9-Goodwell; 10-Cowlington

MY SCORE ______

Oklahoma

Stand Up and Be County-ed!

Score a point for each city you correctly match with its county.

I'm County-ing on You

	City		County
1.	Buffalo	A.	Osage
2.	Pawhuska	B.	Garfield
3.	Miami	C.	Custer
4.	Arnett	D.	Harper
5.	Enid	E.	Lincoln
6.	Stillwater	F.	Payne
7.	Clinton	G.	Ottawa
8.	Chandler	H.	Harmon
9.	Hollis	I.	Tillman
10.	Frederick	J.	Ellis

ANSWERS: 1-D; 2-A; 3-G; 4-J; 5-B; 6-F; 7-C; 8-E; 9-H; 10-I

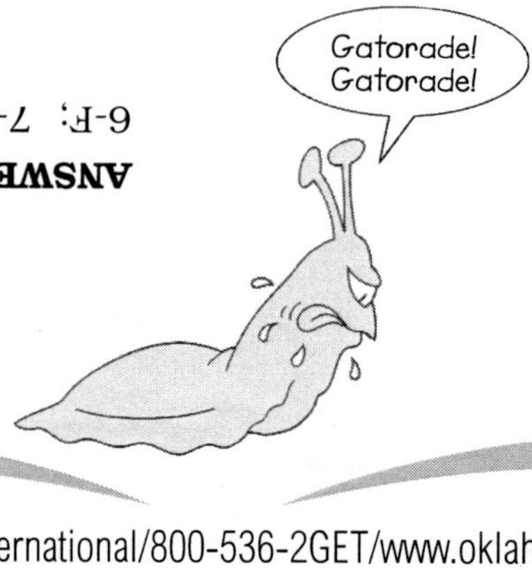

MY ______ SCORE

Oklahoma
Two-Name Places

How many of these two-name places can you figure out? Score a point for each one you match correctly.

Two for the Price of One!

1.	Custer	A.	Autrey
2.	Gene	B.	Oak
3.	Cleo	C.	City
4.	Red	D.	Miami
5.	North	E.	Springs

Help Cleo find her way through the maze to connect with Springs to make up the city of _ _ _ _   _ _ _ _ _ _ _ _.

ANSWERS: 1-C; 2-A; 3-E; 4-B; 5-D

MY SCORE ____

Oklahoma Fast "Fax!"

There are always a few simple facts about our state we are sure we know. See if that's true! Score one point for each correct fact.

FACTS "R" US!

Official Name: ______________________________

Is the ________State/Year: ______________________

Capital: ______________________________

State Nickname: ______________________________

State Motto: ______________________________

State Bird: ______________________________

State Fish: ______________________________

State Tree: ______________________________

State Flower: ______________________________

Greatest Length: ______________________________

Greatest Width: ______________________________

Lowest Point (Name): ______________________________

Highest Point (Name): ______________________________

Number of Counties: ______________________________

ANSWERS: Oklahoma; 46th; 1907; Oklahoma City; Sooner State; "Labor conquers all things"; Scissor-tailed Flycatcher; White or Sand Bass; Redbud; Oklahoma Rose; 230 miles (370 kilometers); 464 miles (747 kilometers); Little River; Black Mesa; 77

MY SCORE ______

Oklahoma

You Have a "Date" with History!

Well, of course you'd rather have a date with that cute kid you're crazy about, but this is geography, remember, so... see how well you score with these dates!

(Sometimes) It Was a Very Good Year!

1. 1812	A. The Missouri Territory is named
2. 1824	B. Dust Bowl drives many Oklahomans out of the state
3. 1541	C. Coronado crosses western Oklahoma in search of riches
4. 1982	D. Rich oil fields discovered near Oklahoma City
5. 1830	E. Forts Gibson and Towson are founded
6. 1930	F. The Five Civilized Tribes sign Reconstruction treaties
7. 1866	G. Indian Removal Act is passed by Congress
8. 1910	H. World oil prices fall, slowing Oklahoma's economy
9. 1895	I. Kickapoo lands are opened
10. 1928	J. The state capital is moved from Guthrie to Oklahoma City

ANSWERS: 1-A; 2-E; 3-C; 4-H; 5-G; 6-B; 7-F; 8-J; 9-I; 10-D

MY SCORE ____

Oklahoma

Festivals!

Jog on down to some of our state's fun festivals and other activities. Score a point for each one you match correctly. Have a great time!

Eat, Drink, and Be Merry!

1. Kolache Festival	A. Guthrie
2. Cheese Festival	B. Prague
3. Bullnanza	C. Claremore
4. American Indian Exposition	D. Norman
5. Red Earth Festival	E. Watonga
6. Will Rogers Day	F. Oklahoma City
7. Robbers Cave Fall Festival	G. Stilwell
8. Strawberry Festival	H. Anadarko
9. Chocolate Festival	I. Bartlesville
10. OK Mozart Festival	J. Wilburton

ANSWERS: 1-B; 2-E; 3-A; 4-H; 5-F; 6-C; 7-J; 8-G; 9-D; 10-I

MY SCORE ______

Oklahoma

Be a Good Sport!

Be a good sport! Score one point each by matching the activity with the most logical place to pursue it!

The Joy of Victory (or the Agony of DA FEET!)

1. Saddle up at the International Finals Rodeo
2. Enjoy a Sooners football game
3. Golf and play tennis
4. Hang on to your horse at the Women's National Finals Rodeo
5. Go rock hunting or spelunking in a cave
6. Attend a Cowboys football game
7. Hike, camp, and picnic
8. Take a float trip down river
9. Cheer on the fastest horse at the races
10. Boat, water-ski, and fish

A. Memorial Stadium

B. Lake Texoma Resort

C. Oklahoma City

D. Ouachita National Forest

E. Guthrie

F. Oklahoma State University

G. Robbers Cave State Park

H. Illinois River

I. Remington Park

J. Tenkiller Ferry Lake

ANSWERS: 1-C; 2-A; 3-B; 4-E; 5-G; 6-F; 7-D; 8-H; 9-I; 10-J

MY ______ SCORE

Oklahoma
The Local Weatherperson–You!

Score one point each if you can fill in the words about our weather. (Do you get a point "weather or not" your answer is correct? NO!)

1. Oklahoma has a __ __ __ __, or temperate, climate.
2. The average temperature in January is __ __°F (__°C).
3. On May 15, 1990, __ __ __ tornadoes and __ __ __ __ __ funnels were sighted in Oklahoma.
4. Most of the time, it's __ __ __ __ __ __ in northern Oklahoma than in the rest of the state.
5. The average temperature in July is __ __°F (__ __°C).
6. The lengthy __ __ __ __ __ __ __ season is important to Oklahoma farmers.
7. Generally, it's __ __ __ in the western portion of the state.
8. Watts suffered Oklahoma's __ __ __ __ __ __ __ temperature in 1930.
9. The record high temperature of __ __ __°F (__ __°C) was at Alva, Altus, Poteau, and Tishomingo.
10. The average annual precipitation in the state is __ __ inches (__ __ centimeters).

ANSWERS: 1-mild; 2-37°F (3°C); 3-six, eight; 4-cooler; 5-82°F (28°C); 6-growing; 7-dry; 8-coldest; 9-120°F (49°C); 10-33 inches (84 centimeters)

MY SCORE ______

Oklahoma

Product Lines!

Match the towns or areas below with a major crop or product. Score a point for each one you match correctly.

1. Gypsum
2. Oil
3. Natural gas
4. Automobiles
5. Lumber
6. Strawberries
7. Salt
8. Peaches
9. Zinc and lead
10. Melons

A. Hugoton

B. The Ozark Plateaus

C. Gypsum Hills

D. Ouachita region

E. Oklahoma City

F. Stratford

G. Ottawa County

H. Harmon and Woods counties

I. Rush Springs

J. Tulsa

ANSWERS: 1-C; 2-J; 3-A; 4-E; 5-D; 6-B; 7-H; 8-F; 9-G; 10-I

MY SCORE ______

Oklahoma

Parks and Such

Oklahoma has a lot of state parks and such!
Score a point for each one you match correctly.

Where the Wild Things Are!

1. Spiro Mounds Archaeological State Park
2. Heavener Runestone State Park
3. The Philbrook Museum of Art
4. Winding Stair Mountain National Recreation Area
5. Myriad Gardens
6. Five Civilized Tribes Museum
7. Chickasaw National Recreation Area
8. Wichita Mountains National Wildlife Refuge
9. Tom Mix Museum
10. Arbuckle Wilderness

A. East-central Oklahoma
B. Muskogee
C. Talihina
D. Oklahoma City
E. Heavener
F. Lawton
G. South-central Oklahoma
H. Tulsa
I. Bartlesville
J. Arbuckle Mountains

ANSWERS: 1-A; 2-E; 3-H; 4-C; 5-D; 6-B; 7-G; 8-F; 9-I; 10-J

MY SCORE ______

Fifty Nifty States!

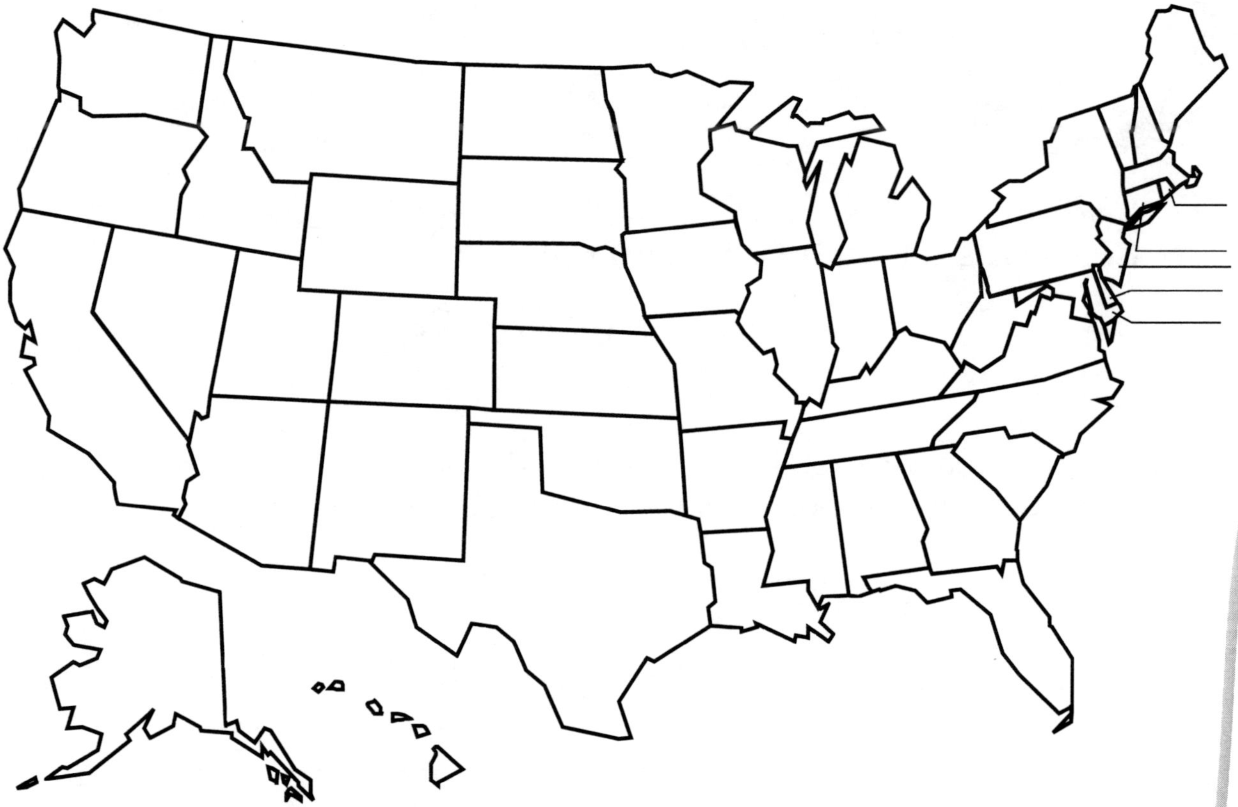

Can you match them all? Write each state's two letter abbreviation in the correct place on the map. See how many you can get right and add 'em up!

Alabama–AL
Alaska–AK
Arizona–AZ
Arkansas–AR
California–CA
Colorado–CO
Connecticut–CT
Delaware–DE
Florida–FL
Georgia–GA
Hawaii–HI
Idaho–ID
Illinois–IL
Indiana–IN
Iowa–IA
Kansas–KS
Kentucky–KY
Louisiana–LA

Maine–ME
Maryland–MD
Massachusetts–MA
Michigan–MI
Minnesota–MN
Mississippi–MS
Missouri–MO
Montana–MT
Nebraska–NE
Nevada–NV
New Hampshire–NH
New Jersey–NJ
New Mexico–NM
New York–NY
North Carolina–NC
North Dakota–ND
Ohio–OH
Oklahoma–OK

Oregon–OR
Pennsylvania–PA
Rhode Island–RI
South Carolina–SC
South Dakota–SD
Tennessee–TN
Texas–TX
Utah–UT
Vermont–VT
Virginia–VA
Washington–WA
West Virginia–WV
Wisconsin–WI
Wyoming–WY

MY SCORE ______

Scavenger Hunt

Have you ever been on a real-life scavenger hunt? Well, here we go! Score two points for each item you find!

Find and Go Seek!

1. Find a newspaper, magazine, or Internet article about an endangered species from our state. List three endangered species.
   ____
   ____

2. Find a picture of the state bird. List the bird's colors and any special characteristics. ______________________________
   ____

3. What is the governor's name? ______________________
   ____

4. Find a newspaper, magazine, or Internet article about a current event. List the date and main idea(s). ____________________
   ____
   ____

5. Listen to a local weather forecast on television or the radio and write down what tomorrow's weather will be. ________________
   ____

MY SCORE ________

Manimals

Score one point for each person or animal you match with the place you might find them!

1. Crows	A. Tallgrass Prairie Preserve
2. Oral Roberts	B. Fort Cobb Recreation Area
3. White-tailed deer	C. McAlester
4. Jim Thorpe	D. Prague
5. Bass and walleye	E. Robert S. Kerr Lake
6. Leona Mitchell	F. Wichita Mountains Wildlife Refuge
7. Bison and Texas longhorns	G. Enid
8. Will Rogers	H. Oklahoma City
9. Reba McEntire	I. Oologah
10. Festival of the Horse	J. Ada

ANSWERS: 1-B; 2-J; 3-A; 4-D; 5-E; 6-G; 7-F; 8-I; 9-C; 10-H

MY SCORE ____

Oklahoma Jog On Down! I

Keep on jogging and see if you can score two points for each correct answer!

Jog On Down, Jog On Down the Road

1. The ___ was the best-known route for cattle drives in Oklahoma.
   - ○ A) East Shawnee Trail
   - ○ B) West Shawnee Trail
   - ○ C) Chisholm Trail

2. Between 1907 and 1910, ____ was the state's capital.
   - ○ A) Guthrie
   - ○ B) Lawton
   - ○ C) Avant

3. The first oil-producing well in Oklahoma was near...
   - ○ A) Chelsea
   - ○ B) Tahlequah
   - ○ C) Tulsa

4. The capital of the Osage Indian Nation is...
   - ○ A) Norman
   - ○ B) Pawhuska
   - ○ C) Okmulgee

5. The Trail of Tears ended at...
   - ○ A) Tahlequah
   - ○ B) Bartlesville
   - ○ C) Muskogee

6. __________ is where the Arkansas, Verdigris, and Grand rivers meet.
   - ○ A) Muskogee
   - ○ B) Tishomingo
   - ○ C) Tulsa

7. In the Creek language, ____ means "bubbling water."
   - ○ A) Pawhuska
   - ○ B) Okmulgee
   - ○ C) Oklahoma City

8. The seven authentically reconstructed villages of Indian City U.S.A. are at...
   - ○ A) Lawton
   - ○ B) Bartlesville
   - ○ C) Anadarko

9. _____ was the result of the Land Run of 1889.
   - ○ A) Oklahoma City
   - ○ B) Tulsa
   - ○ C) Enid

10. Geronimo was imprisoned in the Old Guardhouse at...
    - ○ A) Fort Sash
    - ○ B) Fort Pane
    - ○ C) Fort Sill

MY SCORE ______

ANSWERS: 1-C; 2-A; 3-A; 4-B; 5-A; 6-A; 7-B; 8-C; 9-A; 10-C

Oklahoma

Jog On Down! II

Keep on jogging and see if you can score two points for each correct answer!

Jog On Down, Jog On Down the Road

1. ____ was the result of the last Oklahoma land run in 1901.
   - A) Lawton
   - B) Enid
   - C) Oklahoma City

2. The Mansion of Mattie Beal is located in...
   - A) Anadarko
   - B) Tulsa
   - C) Lawton

3. The geographic center of Oklahoma is 8 miles (13 kilometers) ____ of Oklahoma City.
   - A) north
   - B) south
   - C) east

4. The Gilcrease Museum in ___ has a large collection of Western art.
   - A) Watonga
   - B) Tulsa
   - C) Stillwater

5. ___ in the Choctaw language means "red people."
   - A) Oklahoma
   - B) Washita
   - C) Muskogee

6. The longest river in Oklahoma is the...
   - A) North Canadian River
   - B) Cimarron River
   - C) Salt Fork River

7. The ____ gives Oklahoma its interesting shape.
   - A) Red River
   - B) panhandle
   - C) capital

8. Oklahoma has ____ mountain ranges, even though most people think the state is flat.
   - A) three
   - B) five
   - C) four

9. The Panhandle is only __ __ miles (55 kilometers) long from north to south.
   - A) 34
   - B) 75
   - C) 22

10. Oklahoma borders ___ other states.
    - A) six
    - B) five
    - C) seven

ANSWERS: 1-A; 2-C; 3-A; 4-B; 5-A; 6-A; 7-B; 8-C; 9-A; 10-A

MY SCORE ______

Oklahoma

Jogging Through the State

Let's see how many cool places you've visited. Circle the capital city and all the cities you've visited. Then, label all the really fun spots—like amusement parks, museums, and state parks—you've been to, too! Score one point for each place you locate.

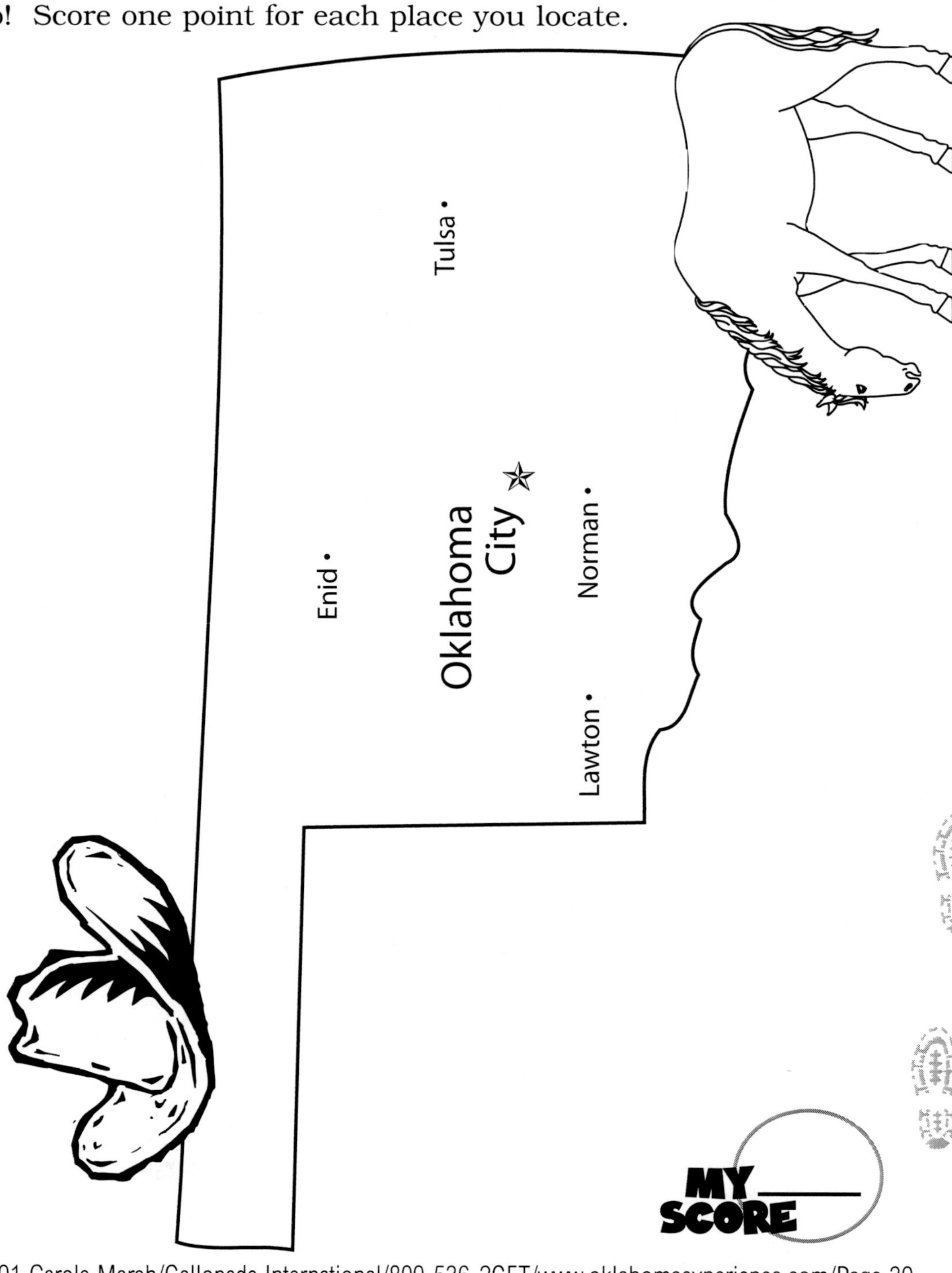

MY SCORE ______

OK, Jogger, How Did You Score?

SOONER OR LATER . . . you're going to have to find out:

If you scored only a few points—you may not be able to find your way home and back! Try and improve your score—it will be easier the second time.

If you scored a few more—well, maybe you really live in Timbuctu? Timbucktoo? Timbuctwo? Try Again!

If you scored lots of points—this book was meant just for you. Don't take those shoes off! Jog, jog again 'til you can improve your score! I know you can do it!!!

Final Score ____________

Make Up Your Own Questions

Here's a place for you to write your own "Jography" questions about places and things in your own hometown.

Quiz your friends! Your parents!! Your teacher!!!

1. ______________________________

2. ______________________________

3. ______________________________

4. ______________________________

5. ______________________________

6. ______________________________

7. ______________________________

8. ______________________________

9. ______________________________

10. ______________________________